A Purr-fect Pair

Read all the books in the

PET RESCUE CLUB

series

ASPCA kids
PET RESCUE CLUB

A Purr-fect Pair

by Rachael Upton
illustrated by Dana Regan

studio fun
INTERNATIONAL

Cover Illustration by Steve James

Studio Fun International
An imprint of Printers Row Publishing Group
A division of Readerlink Distribution Services, LLC
10350 Barnes Canyon Road, Suite 100, San Diego, CA 92121
www.studiofun.com

Studio Fun International is a registered trademark of
Readerlink Distribution Services, LLC.
All notations of errors or omissions should be addressed to
Studio Fun International, Editorial Department, at the above address.

Library of Congress Cataloging-in-Publication Data is available on request.

ISBN 978-0-7944-3811-1
Manufactured, printed, and assembled in Shaoguan, China. SL/09/17
21 20 19 18 17 2 3 4 5 6

**5-7% of the purchase price will be donated to the ASPCA, with a minimum
donation of $50,000 through December 2019.**

To Kai, Bijou, and Nooku, the cats who rescued me.

— R. U.

1

Lolli's Farm

Janey Whitfield had never been this happy before. "Baby goats are the cutest," she said, as she leaned over the fenced pen and petted the baby goat's long ears. The goat bleated softly and wagged its short tail, looking up at Janey with large brown eyes surrounded by long, long lashes. It was so cute, Janey felt like she might melt into the grass.

"They are the cutest," her friend Lolli Simpson agreed. She was sitting on the grass a few feet away, watching Janey

with a big smile on her face. The baby goat belonged to her. Well, really it belonged to her parents, who called themselves "back-to-the-land hippies." They owned a small farm, which meant that Lolli had lots of animals, including sheep, goats, and a dog named Roscoe.

It also meant that sometimes Lolli brought cookies to school that were made of tofu or seaweed. But Janey would eat tofu cookies every day if it meant she got to have a pet of her own. Unfortunately, her father was extremely allergic to everything with fur or feathers, so Janey was usually stuck playing with other people's pets. Not that she minded much, right now.

"You are sublime," she said to the baby goat, whose name was Buttercup. Janey liked to use unusual words whenever and wherever she could. "Sublime" was currently her favorite. "I should have brought my tablet," she said to Lolli. "It has a really nice camera. Then I could have taken pictures of Buttercup for the blog."

Janey's blog had started as a way for other kids around town to share pictures of their pets. Janey thought that if she couldn't have a pet of her own, looking at and posting photos of other people's pets would be the next best thing. Now, however, the blog was mostly used for the club Janey had started with Lolli and two other friends from school, Adam Santos and Zach Goldman. They called themselves the Pet Rescue Club. Their goal was to help animals in need all over town. So far, the four friends had helped dogs, cats, hamsters, and even a pony find happy new homes.

"Buttercup already has a home with me," Lolli pointed out, raising an eyebrow.

"Yeah, but she's so cute. Her cuteness

should be shared with the world," Janey insisted. "Besides, it's been weeks since our last rescue. I should post something so that people don't think I've forgotten the blog."

Lolli got up to join Janey at the fence. She had picked a few handfuls of clover while she was sitting, and handed some to Janey so she could feed Buttercup.

"Maybe you should post an update about one of the animals we helped before," Lolli suggested. "I bet people would love to know how Truman is doing. And he's super-cute, too." Truman was the first dog they'd rescued as a club. He was an adorable little terrier mix who had been adopted by their teacher Ms. Tanaka.

"That's a good idea," Janey agreed.

At school, she could ask Ms. Tanaka for photos of Truman. Still, Janey loved helping animals, and she really wanted a new animal to help. She knew deep down that it was good no animals needed the club's help, because she didn't like to see animals in trouble, but helping animals made her happy, too.

Janey was so lost in thought for a moment that she didn't notice Buttercup had eaten all the clover from her hand, and was now munching on a piece of her long blond hair. "Oh no! That's not food!" Janey exclaimed. She tried to pull back, laughing, and Lolli helped her friend get her hair out of Buttercup's mouth. Buttercup let go and trotted off to the other side of the small pen while Janey tried to wipe the goat drool from her hair.

Lolli was giggling a little. "I guess she thought it was hay."

"It's all right," said Janey, giggling, too. "Even baby goat drool is pretty cute."

"Okay, girls!" came a voice from across the pasture. They looked up to see Lolli's dad, Mr. Simpson, walking toward them and waving. "Let's clear out of the paddock!" he called to them. "I'm going to let the other goats in for feeding time."

Lolli and Janey nodded, and climbed over the fence to the other side, out of the way. Mr. Simpson opened a gate, and two grown-up goats trotted into the paddock and toward the feeder of hay on the other side.

Buttercup bleated at them from her pen. The older goats bleated back, but they seemed much more interested in food than the little goat.

"How long until she can join the rest of the herd?" Lolli asked her dad as he joined the girls at the fence.

"Another week or so," Mr. Simpson replied. "We want to be really sure everyone gets along first. The other goats need to think of Buttercup as a friend, not a stranger.

Otherwise they might hurt her."

"What? But that's so mean!" Janey burst out. Buttercup was much smaller than the adult goats. Why would they hurt her?

"They wouldn't do it to be mean," Mr. Simpson explained. "They'd just be scared. Goats are really protective of their territory. Most animals are. In the wild, they have to defend what they have to survive. Here, we make sure they have everything they need, so it's also up to us to make sure they know they don't have to be scared or fight with one another."

That made a sort of sense to Janey, although she still thought Buttercup was way too small to be scary. "So how do you do that?" she asked. "Help them be friends?"

"Slow and steady does it," said Mr. Simpson. "We're keeping them separate for now, but they can still see and smell each other."

"Animals love to smell each other," Lolli put in, grinning. "Even if they don't always smell great."

"They rely on their smell more than we do," Mr. Simpson agreed. "And by feeding them at the same time, we're also teaching them that there's enough food to go around. Even the most ornery animal can usually be persuaded to make friends, if you take the time to do the introduction right."

At the mention of food, Janey's stomach gurgled loudly. She blushed.

She'd begged her mom to bring her over

early this morning, and it had been a long time since breakfast.

Mr. Simpson laughed. "Why don't you girls head inside to eat? I'll finish up here."

"Let's go, Janey," said Lolli. "The goats will be eating for a while, and I'm starving, too." She looped her arm through Janey's, and together they headed to the house.

. . . .

Lolli's mom must have known they would need a snack, because there was a plate of cookies waiting for them in the living room, and if they had seaweed in them, Janey was too hungry to notice. She and Lolli had soon eaten three each, and Janey was about to reach for a fourth cookie when the phone rang in the kitchen.

Mrs. Simpson answered it, and a moment later called Lolli and Janey from the kitchen. "Girls? It's Kitty, from the Third Street Animal Shelter. She wants to talk to you."

"Oh!" Janey jumped to her feet. Kitty was her favorite worker at the town's animal shelter. She was always patient with Janey and her friends from the club, and happy to let them volunteer there.

Lolli took the phone from her mom, and she and Janey pressed their heads close to the receiver so they could both hear.

"Hello?" said Janey and Lolli in unison.

"Hi, girls!" came Kitty's voice. She was normally calm, but today her voice sounded a little frazzled. "I hate to call you like this, but we have a bit of an emergency at the shelter. I thought I would see if you two are free to come help."

An emergency at the shelter? That was exactly what Janey had been waiting for! Animals needed their help, and Janey was ready to jump into action. "Of course!" she said, forgetting to ask if it was okay with Lolli. Luckily, Lolli was already nodding, too.

"I'll ask my mom for a ride," Lolli said, looking serious. "We'll come as soon as we can."

"Thank you, girls," said Kitty, sounding relieved. "I'll see you soon."

2

Too Many Cats

Janey and Lolli walked into the shelter through the back door marked for volunteers. They'd worried all the way to the shelter about what kind of emergency it was, and now Janey felt ready to burst. She should have asked on the phone, but she'd been so eager to come and help that it hadn't even occurred to her to wonder what the emergency was until after they had already hung up.

"Kitty!" she called as they entered, and then stopped in her tracks, eyes wide, when

she saw the shelter's intake room. "Oh!" she
cried. "Cats!"

On every chair and in every corner
of the room were cat carriers, in stacks
three or four high. There were maybe two
dozen of them. And from the sounds of
meowing, they were full of cats and
kittens. Janey shook her head, unable to

believe what she was seeing and hearing. She hadn't seen the shelter so full since a big tornado had blown through town a couple months earlier. But there hadn't been a tornado today—or any storm at all. It was bright and sunny outside. So what were all these cats doing here?

To double her surprise, their friend and fellow Pet Rescue Club member Zach was there, too, peering into one of the carriers at a litter of kittens. "Hey!" he said to Janey and Lolli, looking up. "Isn't this crazy?"

"I've never heard so many cats in one place," said Lolli, with her hands over her ears to block the meowing. It was true. Even during the storm there hadn't been this many cats, or this much noise.

"You'll get used to it." Zach laughed. "I'm glad you guys came. It's been hard, working by myself. I've been here all morning because Kitty called in Mom to help earlier, and Mom said I couldn't stay home and play video games all day." He rolled his eyes a little, but he didn't look that unhappy to be at the shelter.

Zach's mom, Dr. Goldman, was a veterinarian who owned the Critter Clinic in town. She was always volunteering at the Third Street Animal Shelter, too. She liked animals, and Janey liked her a lot. She liked Zach, too, even if he had a habit of joking around and not taking things seriously enough for Janey's taste.

Kitty and Dr. Goldman came in from the

examination room in the back. Kitty looked just as frazzled in person as she had sounded on the phone. Her normally bouncy blond ponytail was loose and frizzy. But she smiled

when she saw Lolli and Janey. "Hi, girls! Thanks for coming in on such short notice.

As you can see, we're a little overwhelmed."

"No problem," said Lolli.

"We're happy to help," agreed Janey. "But, um . . . where did all these cats come from?" She looked around at the stacks of carriers, still confused and a little amazed.

"The Lakeville shelter," said Dr. Goldman. "They had a big storm overnight, and their shelter building got flooded."

"It wasn't safe for the animals to stay there," Kitty added. "So the other local shelters agreed to take their animals in. Of course, they're a much bigger town than us, so . . . "

"They have a lot more animals," said Lolli, nodding. She was still wide-eyed.

"Exactly," said Dr. Goldman. "This isn't

even all the cats they had in their shelter."

Janey looked around at the cats again, and tried to picture more. The idea was too much. "That's way too many cats," she said finally, shaking her head.

"It's definitely a lot," Kitty said. "And it will probably take a while for the Lakeville shelter's building to be repaired, so it's up to us to feed, house, and try to adopt out all these cats."

Janey nodded. She'd never seen anything quite like this. When the tornado happened, a lot of the animals that came to the shelter already had owners and homes. It had been temporary, but these cats were all in need of good homes. She could see why Kitty had asked for their help.

"Anyway!" Kitty clapped her hands together. "Now that the two of you are here to help Zach, we might finally be able to make some progress. Dr. Goldman is very kindly doing health checks and processing the Lakeville veterinarian paperwork for each and every cat, but I have to help her in the examination room. And poor Mr. Petersen has been on his own in the back room, trying to get kennels ready for our new residents. Do you guys think you can give him a hand?"

"Definitely!" said Janey. "Leave it to us!"

Mr. Petersen was another shelter worker. The Pet Rescue Club didn't see him as often as Kitty—he was usually out "in the field," helping people find lost pets or picking up strays. He waved to them when Kitty showed them to the back room.

"Hey, kids!" he said. "Thanks for coming to help. It's a little bit of a madhouse this morning."

"You can say that again," said Zach, shaking his head, and looking around at the room.

The members of the Pet Rescue Club quickly got organized. Janey carefully filled bowls with food and water, while Lolli laid newspaper and fresh, clean bedding in each kennel. Zach poured litter into the litter boxes, though he let out a loud, clearly fake ah-CHOO! at the dust.

Once some of the kennels were ready, Mr. Petersen helped them move the cats from the carriers into their new temporary homes. Most of the cats were young—almost all of them were kittens, in fact, at which Janey couldn't help but coo. They all seemed tired after their exam, and most quieted down once they were inside the kennels. Several of them curled up and fell right to sleep in their newly made beds.

"Aren't kittens the greatest?" Zach asked. He was petting a trio of little black kittens who were busy investigating their new home. "These little guys are awesome."

"Shh, you'll make Mulberry jealous!" Lolli giggled. Mulberry was Zach's family's cat, a fat orange tabby who loved attention, and got lots of it from Zach's big family. Zach stuck out his tongue at Lolli playfully.

Janey was about to chime in with a

teasing joke of her own, but she was interrupted by a loud, insistent *purr-ROW!* from one of the kennels next to her. She

turned to see a large gray-and-white cat staring at her with one green eye.

For a moment, Janey thought he was winking, but then she realized his left eye wasn't there at all—one side of his face was just smooth gray fur. He didn't seem hurt, though. He meowed again, just as loudly, and rubbed his face against the kennel bars as if saying, "Pet me!"

Just then, Kitty came in from the exam room. "How's it going?" she asked, looking around at the cats. "You guys are the best! Looks like we're nearly done."

"Every kitty is watered and fed," Lolli confirmed.

"But this one is missing an eye," Janey interrupted, unable to help herself.

"What?" asked Lolli and Zach together, rushing over to the cage to see for themselves. The cat didn't notice—he just kept purring and rubbing happily against Janey's fingers.

Kitty had followed them to the kennel, and relaxed when she saw which cat they were talking about. "Oh, that's Chester," she said, reaching through the bars alongside Janey to pet him. "We don't know what happened to his eye exactly, but we can tell it was a long time ago. Dr. Goldman checked him out, and he's just fine."

Janey let out a relieved sigh. "Sublime. I didn't really think you and Dr. Goldman would miss something that important." She smiled up at Chester.

Chester purred louder.

"Most of the cats are just fine, luckily." Kitty sighed, shaking her head a little. "There are just a lot of them."

"I don't think I've seen the kennels this

full since the storm a few months ago," said Mr. Petersen, surveying their handiwork.

Kitty agreed, looking worried. "And just like then, it's going to be a big strain on the shelter's resources."

Janey suddenly had a wonderful idea. One so obvious, she couldn't believe she hadn't thought of it sooner. "Of course!" she cried. "This is the perfect next project for the Pet Rescue Club! I'll write about the cats on my blog."

"I was going to say the same thing," said Lolli, beaming at her friend. "We can get people to donate supplies that way!"

"And help all these cats get adopted," Janey agreed. "I bet people will rush to help!"

Zach looked less certain. "Will people really come adopt a cat just because the shelter is crowded?" he asked doubtfully.

"I mean, there are always cats here."

"We'll think of something," Janey said, feeling much more confident than Zach did. The Pet Rescue Club had always come up with something in the past—she was sure they'd come up with a way to help this time, too.

"Any help the Pet Rescue Club wants to give us is always appreciated," said Kitty, smiling and reaching up to pet Chester again. "And I think I have an idea of how you guys can help spread the word."

3

Zach's Idea

"How many cats?" Adam asked, eyes wide.

It was Monday, and the Pet Rescue Club was having a meeting during school lunch. They were explaining to their fourth member, Adam, about the situation at the shelter. It was unusual for Adam to miss a chance to volunteer, but he had been busy all weekend. Even though he was only nine, Adam was trustworthy enough that he ran his own dog walking business. A lot of people—and dogs—depended on him.

But he was disappointed he'd missed the excitement.

"We're all going back to the Third Street Animal Shelter after school," Zach was saying, with a mouth full of mac and cheese. "My mom is giving us a ride, so you can come, too."

"I'll have to ask my parents, but it should be okay," said Adam, pushing his glasses up. "What's the plan for helping the shelter? Do we have one?" Adam was even more organized than Janey, and liked to have a plan.

"Kitty said we should start with photos," said Janey. She pulled her tablet computer out of her bag. "My tablet has a nice camera, so that should make things simple."

"Seeing how cute the cats are will definitely help," said Lolli, munching on a bag of homemade kale chips. She offered a chip to Janey, and Janey agreed to try just one.

Zach took a few and munched them thoughtfully. "I still don't know if it will help us adopt more cats, though," he said, frowning. "Like I said, there are always cats at the shelter."

"Seeing cute cats always makes me want one," said Janey, wistfully.

"Yeah, but not everyone is like you, Janey. Just because there are extra cats at the shelter doesn't mean there are extra homes for them," Lolli pointed out, putting her chin in her hand.

"We need some kind of an angle to get people's attention. Like, half-off adoption fees. Or buy one cat, get one free!" Zach joked.

Janey groaned and rolled her eyes. She was about to tell Zach to take things more seriously when Adam spoke up. "That's not a bad idea, actually," he said.

"What?" asked Janey.

"What?" Zach repeated.

"Buy one, get one free," said Adam, "or something like that. The Third Street Shelter always does a great job matching pets and people—what a great way to get more a home."

Janey nodded.

"Well, I read in a pet behavior book that some cats are happier in pairs," said Adam. "Especially if they already know each other. They keep each other company and play together. It's harder for them to get bored with another cat around."

"And all of these cats came from the same shelter," said Lolli brightly. "Some of

them even come from the same litter! They definitely already know each other!"

"So if someone wants to adopt one of these cats, we could see if they would want to adopt two instead of one?" asked Janey, warming to the idea.

"If they have time and room for two, why not?" Adam said. "And we could see if the shelter will waive the fees, like Zach said.

Adopt one cat, get the second one free." He paused, then added, "We'll have to ask Kitty first, though. Obviously."

"I mean, it would definitely get cats adopted faster," chuckled Zach. "Like, exactly twice as fast."

"And we can come up with a fun name, like we did with the Walk and Wag!" said Janey, her mind already racing. The Walk and Wag had been a fundraiser the Pet Rescue Club had organized not long ago to help pay for a big dog's knee surgery. It had been enormously successful, and Janey had liked planning an event. This could be just as fun.

"Catpalooza," suggested Adam.

"Double the Love," suggested Lolli.

"Twice the Hairballs," suggested Zach in a serious voice, then burst out laughing.

Janey pretended to throw a wadded-up napkin at Zach, but she laughed, too. One of Zach's jokes had turned out to be a good idea in disguise!

....

After lunch, Lolli and Janey found Ms. Tanaka in the school hallway, and asked her about letting them use the art room to make posters for their adoption idea. She'd let them do the same thing for the Walk and Wag fundraiser, so they were hopeful they'd let her do the same again.

"Well, the Walk and Wag was certainly a good idea," said Ms. Tanaka. "But have you talked to Kitty about your plan yet?"

Janey and Lolli had to admit that they hadn't.

"Get her permission, first," Ms. Tanaka said. "If she says okay . . ." She smiled. "Well, I don't see any reason why you couldn't use the art room again."

"Thank you so much, Ms. Tanaka," said Janey, happily.

"Just make sure it's okay with the shelter before you get ahead of yourselves," Ms. Tanaka warned.

"Definitely," Janey agreed. She'd make sure to ask Kitty about it the minute they got to the shelter that afternoon.

Photo Shoot

As it turned out, though, Janey was too distracted to ask Kitty about it right away, because Kitty had her own surprise waiting for the Pet Rescue Club when they arrived.

When Dr. Goldman dropped off the group at the shelter, Kitty was there to meet them. But instead of bringing them back into quarantine, she brought them into one of the little offices.

Inside, on top of a table, was a blue blanket draped over a frame, making a backdrop like the one Janey posed in front of on school picture day. There were props, like baskets and bows, and toys that jingled and sparkled. It was like the set up for a professional photo shoot.

"What do you guys think?" Kitty asked. "I asked workers from the shelter to bring in extra cat toys from home for the photos."

"This is awesome!" said Zach, diving into one of the baskets with both hands and pulling out a pink feather boa. "Even lazy old Mulberry would flip if he saw all this."

"This is going to be so much fun!" Lolli exclaimed.

"It's sublime, Kitty," Janey agreed. She putting down her backpack and pulling out her tablet, ready to take on the role of cat photographer.

"I thought you kids could use all the help you could get," said Kitty. "A good picture can make all the difference in an adoption."

"Oh yeah," said Adam, nodding. "Remember how Ms. Tanaka didn't want to adopt Truman at first because his picture showed him looking so dirty and sad?" Truman had belonged to a family who had neglected him, and the first pictures Janey had gotten of him had not been very flattering.

"Right!" said Lolli. "But she changed her mind when she saw him cleaned up and in person."

"Exactly," said Kitty. "So let's give these cats and kittens beautiful pictures, and the best chance we can to find good homes."

"We had an idea about that, actually," said Janey, suddenly remembering the Pet

Rescue Club's big idea. She explained it to Kitty. Some of the cats could go in pairs, and the shelter could waive part of the adoption fees. As Janey talked, Kitty started to nod.

"I have to say, your plan might be doable," she said, rubbing her chin. "We've actually done something like that in the past, but it's been a long time. We even had a name for it—we called it Purr-fect Pairs."

It even already had a cute name. Janey felt her excitement rise. "So we can do it?"

"Well," Kitty hesitated, "I have to talk to the other shelter workers. But the shelter is really full. . . . " She rubbed her chin. "I think it's just the right thing to do, and I'm pretty sure that my coworkers will agree." She smiled. "You guys just may have saved the day again."

Janey felt really hopeful that Kitty was right. "Okay, Pet Rescue Club!" she said, holding up her tablet. "Let's get some awesome pictures!"

The photo shoot was even more fun than Janey thought it would be. Kitty brought the cats and kittens into the room one or two or three at a time, and Janey, Lolli, Adam, and Zach took turns at different jobs.

There was a lot to do. Aside from taking pictures, they arranged props for the cats to pose with, and jingled toys to make the cats look toward the camera. Cats jumped into baskets and batted at balls, chased their own tails and rolled over to show their bellies.

Some of them were natural models. They posed and meowed. One or two were nervous, though, and the club took time to calm them and make sure they didn't jump down from the table, or get stressed out by the attention.

Zach took nearly a whole page of photos of the black kittens, because they kept doing more and more cute things. Kitty laughed when she took the kittens back to the kennel.

"Kittens are easy to adopt," she explained when she returned with Chester, the one-eyed cat. "Everyone loves kittens and puppies. It's older animals that are usually harder to find homes for."

Janey bit her lip as Kitty put Chester on the table and he began his usual purr, rubbing against Janey's chin. She stroked his soft fur, looking down at him. "How old is Chester?" she asked.

"Dr. Goldman said about six or seven years old," said Kitty. "He's the oldest cat in the group."

"It's too bad you can't show purring in a picture." Lolli sighed, scratching behind Chester's ear. He leaned his head into her hand, kneading the blanket in front of him and purring even louder.

"We'll just have to make sure he looks really extra-handsome, then," said Janey. She took her tablet back from Zach, and lifted it to get Chester centered on the screen. "Smile for the camera, Chester!"

Chester lifted his head at his name. *"Purr-row?"* he said, waving his long tail, and Janey snapped a picture.

Zach dangled a toy over Chester's head, and the gray-and-white cat raised his paws

to bat at it playfully. Janey snapped another picture. She took extra time, and extra pictures. Soon she'd taken even more photos of Chester than Zach had of the kittens.

"I think that's probably enough," Lolli

said after about fifteen minutes, leaning over Janey's shoulder and staring at the page full of pictures of Chester on the tablet's screen.

"I know, I know," said Janey, sighing. She scrolled through the pictures. "I just want to make sure I get the best picture possible." Plus, if Kitty said it was hard to get older cats adopted, she wondered how hard it was to get an older cat with one eye adopted.

Finally, even Janey had to admit that she'd taken enough photos of Chester when he lay down in the middle of the table and began to fall asleep. No jingling toys or belly pokes could get him to stand back up. He just purred tolerantly and kept his eye closed. He was clearly done being a model for the day.

Kitty brought Chester back to his kennel,

and the Pet Rescue Club picked up the props and cat toys, returning the room to normal before Dr. Goldman came to pick them up.

Before they left, Janey stopped by Chester's kennel one last time. He was still sleepy, and squeezed his eye shut as she stroked behind his ear, giving her a soft "purr-row."

"Don't worry, Chester," she whispered. "I'll help you find a loving home. I promise!"

5

Surprise Arrival

"What about this one?" Janey asked, holding out her tablet to Adam.

"It's a good picture," said Adam. "But they're almost all good pictures, Janey."

"You should pick one and move on," said Zach, munching on a seaweed cracker. "If you keep changing your mind, we'll never finish the blog entry."

Lolli's dog, Roscoe, whined at Zach, his eyes on the cracker in his hand. Roscoe was a large mixed breed—part Labrador, part rottweiler, and part who-knew-what. Zach held the cracker out of his reach. "Sorry, boy," he said. "These are weirdly tasty, and they're also all mine."

The Pet Rescue Club had met at Lolli's house. Janey had heard from Kitty that the Purr-fect Pairs event was on for the next weekend. Potential adopters would be encouraged to adopt cats and kittens in twos. If they did, the shelter would waive the adoption fee for one of the cats.

Janey wanted to post on her blog to promote the event. They had more than enough pictures of all the adoptable cats, and the club had already made posters to hang up around town, just like they had for the Walk and Wag. Updating the blog was the next step.

If only Janey could decide on which pictures to use.

"May I see?" asked Lolli, reaching for the tablet. Janey handed it over and Lolli scanned the pages of photos.

"This one," she said at last, tapping one to make it full size and handing the tablet back. Chester was sitting, his paws tucked in front of him. He was looking at the camera with his one big green eye. He looked regal, like a jungle cat.

Janey nodded. "Okay. This one." Then she frowned, scrolling further down. "Or maybe . . . this one?"

Adam and Zach groaned. Part of the reason they were at Lolli's house was also so they could meet Buttercup, the baby goat.

Instead, they'd been stuck choosing pictures for almost an hour.

"Sorry," Janey said, feeling a little exasperated that the others didn't share her sense of just how important this was. She picked the picture Lolli had suggested and handed the tablet to Zach, folding her arms.

"I'm just trying to make sure Chester has a really good chance of being adopted this weekend."

Lolli hugged Janey. "It will be okay. When people come to the shelter and meet Chester, they'll love him. He's really sweet."

Zach's fingers tapped at Janey's tablet. He was better with computers than anyone else Janey knew, and she always let him look over the Pet Rescue Club's blog posts before she made them. "Speaking of sweet . . . ," Zach said, and held up the tablet to show a picture of one of the black kittens from the shelter. "I'm going to ask Mom if we can adopt her. Mulberry probably needs a friend, too, right?"

"Mulberry has lots of company," Janey

said. "You have two brothers, and he gets lots of attention from them. And your parents. And you."

"Shh, you'll ruin my plan to adopt Blackberry." Zach grinned. "See? Her name even matches Mulberry's."

"Because you named her," Adam pointed out, bumping his knee into Zach's leg and grinning back.

"It's a good name!" Zach insisted. He tapped at the screen a little longer, then handed the tablet back to Janey. "Here you go. Blog post is all ready to go."

Janey looked it over one more time, then hit the "post" button. She exhaled, then put the tablet down. "Okay! Let's go see Buttercup."

Zach jumped to his feet, and Roscoe,

who was still hoping for a cracker, jumped up with him to follow them outside. "It's about time!"

"That is not a baby goat," Adam said a moment later.

They were standing in the door of Lolli's barn, looking down at a little white kitten. It was rubbing up against Mr. Simpson's ankles, and meowed when it saw the Pet Rescue Club, trotting toward them with its tail held high.

"Oh my gosh!" said Lolli, dropping to her knees and scooping up the kitten. "Dad, where did it come from?"

"I'm not sure," Mr. Simpson admitted. "She was just here when I came to check on Buttercup a few minutes ago. It looks like she's been outside for a while."

"Poor little thing!" Janey petted the kitten, who closed her eyes and purred and purred, rubbing her head on Janey's hand. Up close, Janey could see what Mr. Simpson meant. The kitten was dirty and skinny. Still, she seemed too friendly to be a stray. "Maybe she's someone's runaway pet?"

"Maybe so," said Mr. Simpson. "Or maybe she was abandoned out here."

Lolli put the kitten down on the floor of the barn, and the kitten resumed walking around their feet and rubbing on their legs.

"Just what we need," said Zach, crouching to pet her, too. "Another cat." He didn't really sound that upset, though. He smiled when the kitten rolled over onto her back and started chewing on his fingers. "Oh, wait, Roscoe!"

Roscoe had followed the kids into the barn, and had spotted the kitten. He leaned his big head down to sniff at her. His mouth was nearly as big as her whole body. But the kitten just reached up with her paws and started licking Roscoe's nose.

Roscoe made a confused sound, but started wagging his tail and panting. It was clear the kitten was in no danger from him.

"False alarm," said Zach, obviously relieved.

"Boy, she's friendly." Adam started petting the kitten as well. "What are you going to do with her?"

"Well, first I was going to ask around the neighborhood to see if I could find her owners," Mr. Simpson said, sighing. "If not, I thought I'd take her to the Third Street Animal Shelter."

At that, the club members looked at each other in dismay.

"You can't bring her to the shelter, Dad," exclaimed Lolli. "It's already crowded with cats, remember?"

"Oh, right!" Mr. Simpson slapped his own forehead, laughing a little. "I don't know how I forgot. You kids have been so busy with the . . . what is it? The Twin Tails event?"

"Purr-fect Pairs," Janey corrected him. "And once it's over, I'm sure there will be room at the shelter again."

"Could we keep her until then?" Lolli asked, hopefully. "She's so sweet. Even Roscoe likes her. I could keep her in my bedroom, and I know how to make a temporary litterbox, and it would only be for a few days . . . " She gave her dad a pleading look. The kitten mewed and looked up at Mr. Simpson with big blue eyes.

"Okay, okay," Mr. Simpson chuckled. He was usually pretty easy-going when it came to fostering—he'd once even let Lolli foster a pony on the farm. "We'll have to take her to the vet first to see if she needs vaccines or deworming. But you know I can't resist your puppy-dog eyes. If I can't find her owner myself, we'll keep her here until after the Purr-fect Pairs event. But!" He pointed at Lolli firmly. "You have to be completely responsible for her until then, Lolli. Can you do that?"

"Absolutely!" said Lolli.

"No fair," said Zach. "You get a kitten and a baby goat?"

Lolli laughed, picking the kitten back up. "Just lucky, I guess. Speaking of which! C'mon guys, meet Buttercup."

Janey was happy to see that Buttercup was finally in with the other two goats, and no one seemed to be fighting at all. Adam and Zach oohed and ahhed over her beautiful black and white coat, feeding her clover and scratching behind her ears.

The kitten, it turned out, was friendly to people and dogs, but had no interest in goats. She seemed happy to stay snuggled in Lolli's arms and fall asleep. She stayed that way until the Pet Rescue Club's parents came to the farm to pick them up an hour later. Janey thought that the kitten must have been on her own a long time, to be so tired. It didn't seem likely that she came from anywhere nearby.

Instead, Janey had a feeling she would be seeing the kitten again soon, at the Third Street Animal Shelter.

6

Purr-fect Pairs

It had been a busy week for Janey and the rest of the Pet Rescue Club. In addition to keeping up with all of the regular stuff they had to do, like school, homework, and chores, they'd been preparing nonstop for the Purr-fect Pairs event.

Lolli also had the new kitten to take care of—she'd even e-mailed some photos to Janey, knowing how much Janey loved to look at pictures of cute animals. Lolli had named her "Elsa," and Janey thought the name was sublime. They both thought the name suited the kitten somehow.

Janey had also gotten a lot of messages from the blog about the shelter's cats. It was almost more than she expected. Even people who said they couldn't adopt still e-mailed and promised to donate so that the shelter had extra support while it was extra full.

All of this made Janey really hopeful that the Purr-fect Pairs event would go well. She woke up at the crack of dawn on the morning of the event and could barely eat breakfast. She hadn't felt this excited since the Walk and Wag.

Her mom drove her to the shelter an hour before it opened. Janey and the rest of the club had agreed to come a little early to help set up for the event before it started. An hour was probably not "a little," but Janey was too impatient to wait any longer.

Kitty and another shelter worker were already inside, setting up chairs and tables when Janey came in through the volunteer door.

"Hi!" Janey said breathlessly. "Is anyone else here yet?"

"You're the first," said Kitty cheerfully. "But I'm sure your friends won't be far behind. In the meantime, can you sweep the cat room?"

"Of course!" Janey bounced back toward the first cat room, unable to keep from skipping a little in her excitement. The cat room was full, of course, and there was a

lot of hair and litter to sweep.

As Janey cleaned, lots of cats ran around her feet, chasing toys or begging for attention. Chester circled her leg, and Janey couldn't resist bending down to hug him. Some of the other cats from the Lakeville shelter had been moved to the cat room, too—including Blackberry, Zach's favorite kitten.

"Hi, Chester," Janey said to the cat. "We're going to find you a home today! Aren't you excited?" Chester purred and licked her chin, and Janey giggled.

Truthfully, though, Janey was a little worried about Chester. Although she'd gotten a lot of messages about the cats, only one message had been about Chester. And it had been a comment by someone who said his missing eye made him look "mean."

"But you aren't mean," Janey said to Chester, who purred in her arms. "You're the sweetest cat I've ever met. I'm sure someone will see that today."

"I thought you were supposed to be cleaning," said Zach. He had come in without Janey noticing, and was already making a beeline for the little black kitten that he was so fond of.

"I am! I was just taking a kitty-cuddle break." Janey grinned at Zach. "Any luck convincing your mom to let you adopt Blackberry?"

"No," Zach sighed as he picked up the kitten and held her under his chin. "She said that Mulberry gets plenty of attention already, and I need to be older before she'll let me have my own cat. So Blackberry will have to find another home." He sounded so genuinely sad that Janey felt sorry for teasing him before.

"I'm sorry," she said. "I know we can make sure Blackberry gets an amazing home, too."

"Definitely," Zach agreed, nodding as Blackberry put her paws on Zach's nose. "It's okay, buddy. We'll make sure you get a great home."

It wasn't long before Lolli and Adam arrived at the shelter. With all four of them working together, the cat room and cat kennels were quickly cleaned and ready for potential adopters.

The Pet Rescue Club emerged from the back of the shelter. Kitty waved to them and pointed out the glass front door. To Janey's surprise, there were already people lined up outside. Some were even holding printouts of cat photos Janey and the others had taken.

"It worked!" Janey squeaked in excitement.

"I'd say it did," Kitty agreed. She glanced up at the clock on the wall. "And it's nine o'clock. Let's get this show on the road."

She walked to the doors and unlocked them to let the waiting people inside.

. . . .

Zach was sitting in on the adoption process for Blackberry, just to make sure that she was going to a good home. He had been sort of hoping that no one would come to adopt Blackberry, and give him another chance to convince his mom to let him adopt the kitten.

Unfortunately for Zach, Kitty's prediction that the kittens would be adopted most quickly turned out to be true. And, Zach had to admit, the family who were interested in adoping Blackberry seemed great. The Davidsons had seen Blackberry's picture on Janey's blog, and had come to the shelter specifically to adopt her.

Right now, their daughter Cassie was

sitting on the floor with Blackberry, waving a piece of cloth back and forth for her to chase.

"We're so excited," said Mrs. Davidson. "We saw the blog and she just seemed perfect as a companion for our cat Marshmallow." She looked up at Zach with a wistful smile. "We actually adopted Marshmallow from the Third Street Animal Shelter a few years ago, before Cassie was born, and he's been absolutely wonderful. But he's getting older, and a kitten might be just what he needs to make him feel young again." She smiled down at Blackberry. "And we've always wanted another cat for Cassie to grow up with."

"Kittens can get along well with older

cats," said Kitty, who was helping Mr. Davidson finish the adoption paperwork. "And I'm so glad you came back to the shelter to adopt from us again! Just make sure to introduce them slowly. It's good to start them in separate rooms for a week or two so they can get used to each other's scent before they meet face-to-face.

"I looked up some tips online," said Mrs. Davidson, smiling. "Blackberry will stay in Cassie's room for the first few days. Marshmallow is a pretty easy-going cat. I think he'll do just fine."

"Cassie has been asking for a kitten for a while," Mr. Davidson admitted. "She saw Blackberry on the blog and just fell in love. We thought we should at least come to see her."

"And seeing them playing together . . . I'm convinced she's the right cat for us," Mrs. Davidson agreed. "We'll take good care of her."

"I think you guys will really love Blackberry," Zach said. "She's a really sweet and gentle kitten." He didn't say that he would have liked to be the one taking Blackberry home, but the Davidsons seemed like the next best thing.

He bent down to pet the little black kitten. "Goodbye, Blackberry," he said softly. "You're gonna love your new home."

"I promise she will," said Mr. Davidson, smiling, and Zach felt a little better.

He got up to see how the other members of the Pet Rescue Club were doing. So far, it seemed like the event had been the success they had been hoping for. Some cats and kittens were getting adopted alone, like Blackberry, but many of them were getting adopted in pairs.

Zach found Janey sitting on a chair in a corner of the room. He followed her gaze and saw that she was watching a couple play with Chester. The big cat was rolling on his back in front of them, meowing his loud, happy "*purr-row!*" The couple seemed entertained, but when a kitten ran in front of them, they quickly lost interest in Chester, picking up the kitten instead. After a moment, they walked to one of the adoption tables, the kitten in their arms.

"No one will give him enough of a chance," said Janey, sadly. "Every time I think someone's about to adopt him, they choose a kitten."

Zach sat down next to her. "There are a lot of kittens," he pointed out. "Maybe we just need to be patient."

"Maybe . . . " Janey sighed. "I just feel so bad for him. He's really trying his hardest."

"Hey," Zach said, poking Janey's shoulder. "You tried your hardest, too. And if they can't see how awesome a cat he is, then they don't deserve him anyway, right?"

Janey looked like she might cry for a minute. Then she rubbed at her eyes, sniffled, and poked Zach back. "Yeah. You're right." She let out another long sigh, then looked around. "Did Blackberry get adopted already?"

"Yep." Zach pointed out the Davidsons, who seemed to just be wrapping up the paperwork. "To a good home, too."

"I know you wanted her," said Janey. "I'm sorry."

"It's okay." Zach shook his head. "As long as Blackberry is happy, I'm happy." And he was surprised to find he meant it. Being in the Pet Rescue Club meant meeting lots of animals he wished he could adopt himself. But working hard and seeing an animal go to a loving home was a great feeling, too.

7

Special Chester

By the end of the day, lots of cats and kittens had been adopted into new, loving homes. The cat room wasn't empty, but it was definitely a lot quieter than before.

Except for Chester, who was purr-rowing loudly and happily as Janey rubbed under his chin. Despite her best efforts, and despite Chester being his very extra-friendliest self to every person who'd come in the door, he was still at the shelter. No one had come to adopt him.

"I'm sorry, Chester," Janey said quietly. "I thought for sure we'd find you a home today." She bit her lower lip.

"Don't be so down, Janey," said Lolli, sitting next to her. "Just because Chester didn't get adopted doesn't mean the event wasn't amazing. We helped find homes for so many cats today."

"Kitty says it's a record number of cat adoptions for a single day," called Adam, who was helping Kitty fold chairs.

"I just feel like I did something wrong," Janey said unhappily. "Maybe if I took better pictures, or tried to hide his missing eye . . ."

"Nah, we should emphasize it," said Zach, rubbing Chester just above his tail. "Give him an eye patch, and change his name to Captain Chester. I bet everyone would want a pirate cat."

Janey hesitated, and actually thought about it for a minute.

"I'm kidding," Zach said, raising an eyebrow.

"I know, I know," Janey said, feeling sadder. "I just wish he'd been one of the cats who found a home today, that's all."

"Janey, you guys did an amazing thing for the shelter," said Kitty, walking over to her. "Don't blame yourself for Chester. He'll be fine. He hasn't been here all that long, and like I said, it can sometimes take a little longer for older cats to get adopted. Especially ones with a little extra wear and tear." She smiled down at Chester affectionately. "He'll find a loving home soon enough."

He will, thought Janey. Because I won't give up until he does.

The Pet Rescue Club finished helping to clean, and then waited for their parents to pick them up. Lolli's dad was the first one to arrive, and to everyone's surprise, he had a cat carrier in his hands when he did.

"Is that Elsa?" Lolli asked, running up to her dad.

"Who's Elsa?" asked Zach, following her. Janey supposed Lolli hadn't had time to tell him—they'd all been really busy.

"Remember the kitten who turned up at our farm?" Lolli said. "We couldn't find her owners after all. We even brought her to Dr. Goldman to have her scanned for a microchip. Nothing."

"I talked to Kitty on the phone," said Mr. Simpson. "She said you guys helped lots of cats get adopted today. I'm guessing that means there's finally room for this little one?"

"There certainly is, Mr. Simpson," said Kitty, waving him in and peering into the carrier. "What a little beauty!"

"I have vet paperwork for her, too," said Mr. Simpson. "I hope you don't mind that I went ahead and paid for her to have her vaccinations."

"We don't mind at all. And she's been kept in quarantine at your house, so we can put her into the cat room right away," said Kitty. "You've saved us a lot of trouble by doing all this."

"Well, with all that my daughter does, I feel like I have to help any way I can," said Mr. Simpson, putting the carrier down on the floor and starting to fill out paperwork.

"You didn't want to keep her?" Zach

asked Lolli, as Kitty and her dad chatted.

"Well, yeah," said Lolli, "of course I did. But we have so many animals on the farm, and we just got Buttercup. It's already a lot of work. A new kitten would just be too much."

"I guess that's true," said Adam. "You guys have so many animals, you have to think carefully before you add a new one."

Lolli nodded. "I'm sad she's going, but I know she'll find a loving home with someone else."

Probably before Chester does. The thought popped into Janey's head before she could stop it, and it made her feel sad, despite all the good they'd done that day.

8

Picture Perfect

Days passed before Janey could go back to the shelter. She wound up having to go by herself—Lolli and Zach had chores to do, and Adam had dogs to walk. But Janey couldn't stay away. She wanted to see how Chester was doing, and Lolli had also asked her to check on how Elsa was settling in. She got permission from her mom to walk to the animal shelter after school, and almost ran all the way there.

Kitty looked up from the desk when

Janey came in. She didn't look surprised to see her. "Hey, girl!" she called, winking. "Ready to scoop some litter boxes?"

"Sure am!" Janey replied. Even the stinkiest jobs at the animal shelter were still a chance to spend time with the animals.

"I swear you're the only kid I know who doesn't mind cleaning litter boxes." Kitty chuckled, waving Janey back toward the cat room. "I'll give you a hand, come on."

Janey followed her. When Kitty pushed the door of the first cat room open, she looked around, seeing if she could spot Chester or Elsa.

To her surprise, they were together by one of the cat towers. Elsa lay on her side next to Chester, his long tail in her paws, grooming him happily. Chester looked happy, too—his one green eye was closed and his purr was loud enough to hear several feet away.

As Janey watched, Elsa nipped the end of Chester's tail, and then ran away. Chester chased her, pouncing on her and pinning her to the floor with one big paw. For a split second, Janey was scared that he might hurt her, but he only licked the top of her head and then flopped over onto his side.

"Wow!" Janey said, eyes wide.

"Yeah, I'm surprised, too," said Kitty, beaming. "The first day Elsa got here, she went right over to Chester like they were already best friends. They've been basically inseparable ever since." She took her phone out of her pocket and showed Janey a few photos she'd taken: Elsa and Chester eating together at a food bowl; Elsa and Chester sharing a toy; Chester grooming the side of Elsa's face while Elsa closed her eyes happily.

"Too bad my phone's camera isn't that good," she added. "Otherwise I'd send them to you for your blog."

"Oh my gosh, those are awesome!" Janey looked from the camera to the two cats. They looked back up at her and meowed. Chester got up, put his paws on her knee, and rubbed his head against her leg as Elsa chewed on her shoelaces. Janey giggled, almost falling over.

"I've never seen anything like it," said Kitty. "It's like they've known each other forever."

"Lolli's dad said you have to introduce animals to each other slowly," Janey said, watching in amazement as the two cats began to wrestle playfully.

"Usually that's the case," Kitty agreed. "Most cats have to learn to get along, just like people. We're careful not to let anyone fight, but usually a new cat will avoid all the other cats in the cat room for a while. But sometimes two animals can just . . . click. I've never seen it happen this fast, though."

Janey nodded and petted both of them for a minute more. If Chester didn't have a home yet, at least he'd found a friend. She could be happy about that.

Finally, she stood up and brushed off her hands on her jeans. Time to get to work. As always, there was a lot to do. Kitty helped her scoop litter boxes, then left to finish up some paperwork in the office. On her own, Janey swept the floor, refilled the water bowls, and wiped off the cat furniture.

And every move she made, Elsa and Chester followed behind her. They batted at toys and wrestled, or stepped on her feet to stop her from walking and to get her to pet them. Janey didn't mind a bit, of course—it just meant it took a little bit longer than usual to do the cleaning.

It was too bad Elsa hadn't been at the shelter during the Purr-fect Pairs event, Janey thought as she worked. She and Chester would have made a perfect purr-fect pair themselves.

At last, Janey finished cleaning. The cat room was spotless. And, she realized, Chester and Elsa had disappeared. They must have tired themselves out playing, she thought.

She put the duster she had been using down on a windowsill and went looking for them. She had to say good-bye before she left.

It took her a little while to find them. And when she did, she couldn't believe her eyes.

Elsa and Chester were sleeping together on one of the pet beds. That wasn't surprising. What was surprising was the way they were sleeping.

The two cats were cuddled close, lying nose-to-nose and tail-to-tail, their backs curved just so. Looking at them from above, they formed a shape that looked almost exactly like a heart.

Janey got a wonderful idea suddenly.

Quietly, she snuck out of the room on her tiptoes, and went to the office, where she'd stashed her backpack. She pulled out her tablet computer, and returned to the cat room, just as quietly.

To her relief, Elsa and Chester hadn't moved.

Janey opened the camera app on her tablet and lifted it up, making sure both cats were in frame. Then she snapped a few pictures. The first couple of photos came out blurry, but the third was just right. Elsa and Chester didn't just look kind of like a heart—they looked exactly like a heart. It was just what she had been hoping for.

"Kitty!" Janey ran out of the cat room, holding her tablet against her chest. "Kitty, Kitty!"

Kitty stuck her head out of the office.

"Janey? Is something wrong?"

"Nothing's wrong! Everything's sublime!" Janey beamed, holding the tablet up for Kitty to see.

"Whoa!" Kitty gazed at the photo on

the screen. "Is that Elsa and Chester? Did you take this picture?"

Janey nodded. "I saw them sleeping in a heart shape, and I remember what you said about photos being important, and . . . I think this might be the one that gets Chester adopted."

Kitty agreed. "He looks so adorable here. And Elsa, too!"

"Yeah." Janey smiled. "I was wondering—could we maybe let them be adopted as a pair? Like last weekend? Like you said, they get along so well."

Kitty nodded slowly. "I think that is doable. I mean, with a picture this great, how could I say no?"

Janey jumped for joy. "Thank you, thank you!"

"I'm guessing this photo will be going up on the blog?" Kitty smiled.

"Yep!" Janey beamed. "As soon as I talk to the other members of the Pet Rescue Club."

9

Second Chances

"This is the cutest picture I think I've ever seen," Adam said, staring at the tablet screen. Janey had convinced the Pet Rescue Club to hold an impromptu meeting during recess the next day. They were sitting on the bleachers together, looking at the amazing photo.

Janey noticed Zach was looking a little longingly toward the soccer field, where some of the other boys were playing. But he quickly looked back, grinning his approval at the picture.

"I'm so glad that Elsa is Chester's best friend," Lolli said happily. "And Kitty said they could be adopted together?"

"Yep! Two-for-one, just like the event last weekend," Janey confirmed. "As long as they go to the same home. I thought it would be best if we all wrote the blog post together, though. Especially you, Lolli, since your family fostered Elsa for a little while. You know her better than I do."

"And you know Chester pretty well," said Lolli, nodding enthusiastically. "You've spent more time with him than we have. We can write a great blog post together."

"What about us?" Zach asked, holding up a hand like they were in class.

"Of course I need you guys to help."

Janey laughed. "Purr-fect Pairs wouldn't have happened at all without you. And now we have a chance to get Chester and Elsa a home together. We just have to make this blog post perfect."

"You mean purr-fect." Adam grinned.

Zach groaned. "I'm getting tired of that pun."

"I still think it's cute," Lolli chimed in.

"Okay, Adam, write this down, then," said Zach, as he stood up, striking a dramatic pose. "This is the tale of Chester the pirate cat, captain of the good ship Meow-Meow, hero of the seven seas, eater of sardines—"

"Zach!" Lolli interrupted, giggling. "I don't think that's what Janey had in mind."

"No," Janey snorted, covering her mouth to keep from giggling as well. "But I think you should tell Ms. Tanaka all about Captain Chester next time we have creative writing."

"Okay, okay," Zach sat back down, but he was grinning ear-to-ear, and no longer stealing glances at the soccer field.

Janey smiled around at her friends. She thought again how lucky she was to have the Pet Rescue Club—to have friends who loved animals like she did, and who were happy to give up a recess to help animals in need.

"Let's tell it like a story," she said, thoughtfully. "But a real one. About how two cats who didn't know each other at all became the best of friends."

With all four friends working together,

Chester and Elsa's story took shape. They even added some information about the benefits of older cats, like that they're already litter trained! It took all recess, and about half of lunch, but eventually they had a blog post that they were proud of. It told all about the two cats' rather sad backgrounds, but also explained how happy they were together, and how the shelter wanted to keep them together so that they could stay friends.

Janey promised to post it as soon as she got home.

. . . .

After she hit "post" on the blog that afternoon, Janey couldn't help but be anxious. The photo was amazing. The blog

post was amazing. But would anyone read it? She kept her tablet with her all evening, watching it with her e-mail open while she did her homework, brushed her teeth, and put on her pajamas. She could barely even pay attention to her favorite show, because she kept glancing down at the screen in her lap.

She would have brought it with her to the table at dinner if her mother hadn't forbidden it. "A watched in-box never chimes," she joked as she served Janey some peas.

"The picture and the post are beautiful," Janey's dad added. "You guys did a great job. Just relax."

Janey was not relaxed. After dinner, she stared at her empty e-mail folder until her mom finally made her turn the tablet off and go to bed. Even then, she tossed and turned for a little while, visions of heart-shaped cats in her head, before she finally managed to fall asleep.

She woke up to her mom gently shaking her shoulder, which was unusual. It was Saturday, and her mom usually let her sleep in a little bit on the weekend. She almost never woke Janey up unless there was something to do. Janey started to mumble something about the time, but her mom interrupted her.

"Honey? I think you might want to check your e-mail," her mom whispered, looking bemused.

Janey sat up, looking blearily at her mom, then down at the tablet she was holding out. The tablet's e-mail program showed a little number next to the icon, letting her know how many e-mails she had.

Right now, the number read fifty-eight.

As Janey watched, it clicked up to fifty-nine. She rubbed her eyes and blinked, thinking maybe she was seeing things. Still fifty-nine. Janey squeaked in surprise, thoroughly awake now.

"I'd say your photo worked," Janey's mom chuckled as Janey tapped the icon to open her e-mail.

She scanned the subject lines of the messages in her in-box. Every single e-mail was about Chester and Elsa! Some were just talking about how cute the photo was, but Janey could see many messages just on the first page, asking about adopting both cats.

"I have to call Kitty!" Janey said, looking up at her mom with a giant smile on her face.

"Kitty already called you earlier this morning," Janey's mother replied. "She said the shelter had half a dozen calls about your cats this morning. People from as far away as the next county want to adopt Chester and Elsa. That's why I turned your tablet on and woke you up."

"But how?" Janey was amazed. Her blog had been helpful in getting attention and help for animals in the past, but never this much, and never this fast.

"Apparently," her mother explained, "a reporter from the local news has been following your blog. He remembered your club from back when you all helped with the big storm, and thought it would be a good idea to keep an eye on you guys, in case you did something else amazing." She smiled. "He thought the photo was really cute, too. He put it and a link to your blog on the website this morning. He called Kitty, too. He said the photo went kind of viral."

"So Chester and Elsa are famous!" Janey hugged the tablet to her chest and bounced in place on her bed, unable to contain her excitement. "That. Is. Sublime! I have to tell everyone—Adam and Lolli and Zach, I mean—and I have to call Kitty back—oh my gosh, there's so much to do!"

"Why don't we start with getting dressed and having breakfast?" her mom suggested. "Your dad is making pancakes, and I think Internet fame can wait until after you've eaten."

Janey called Kitty almost as soon as she had swallowed her last bite of pancake. Kitty sounded frazzled again, but in a good way. "The phone has been ringing off the hook all morning. The shelter director even said that we could extend the Purr-fect Pairs promotion to this weekend, too. The reporter who posted your photo is going to write a story about it for the news website."

"I can't believe it," said Janey, feeling dizzy.

"Neither can I," Kitty admitted. "It's amazing. And we have a dozen people interested in adopting Chester and Elsa."

"A dozen?" Janey cried. "That's so many!"

"It is," Kitty agreed. "Do you have time to come by the shelter today?"

"Yes!" Janey did a little dance on her end of the phone.

Kitty laughed, as if she was picturing Janey's victory dance. "Okay. I'll see you later today. And the rest of the Pet Rescue Club, too, I hope!"

10

Happy Homes

The shelter was crowded again, but with people instead of cats. There were even more people than there had been the previous weekend.

"We aren't going to run out of cats, are we?" Zach whispered to Lolli.

"Maybe?" Lolli whispered back. "I don't think that would be so bad, though."

"It'd be unprecedented," Adam said. "But why are we whispering?"

Janey could hear their quiet conversation, but tried to ignore it for now. Lots of people had come to adopt Chester and Elsa—but since only one family could adopt one pair of cats, many families had stayed to meet and adopt other cats. Mr. Petersen had told the Pet Rescue Club an hour ago that they had officially adopted more than half the cats in the entire shelter.

As great as that news was, though, Janey had to focus. Kitty had asked her to sit in on their adoption interview, and Janey intended to take the responsibility seriously. She looked back to the young couple who were holding Chester and Elsa in their laps.

She already really liked Sam and Isabel. They hadn't just been the first ones to call the Third Street Animal Shelter to ask about

Elsa and Chester. They'd also been the first ones in line when the shelter opened, and Elsa and Chester hadn't moved from their laps since they sat down.

"We just moved into town last week," Sam was saying to Kitty, rubbing Elsa under the chin. "Otherwise we would have been here last weekend, too."

"Our cat Michou died a few months before we moved," Isabelle put in sadly as she stroked Chester's fur. "He was sixteen, and I'd had him since I was in high school."

"Sixteen?" Janey said in amazement. That was almost twice as old as she was.

Isabel nodded, smiling a little. "It took a long time for me to feel ready to adopt another cat, but Sam and I decided we'd get two once we moved to our new house. I was so sad when I found out we'd just missed the Purr-fect Pairs event!"

"Lucky for us, these guys convinced you to give it another go," said Sam, looking fondly down at Chester. "When I saw that photo, I woke Izzy up to show her."

"I was so mad at Sam until I saw the cats," Isabel laughed. "Then I totally forgave him. Especially once I saw the other photo of Chester."

"Really?" That piqued Janey's curiosity. "The one from the blog post before?"

"Oh yes! As soon as I saw him, I knew we had to try to adopt him and Elsa." Isabel beamed as she reached into her purse and pulled out her phone. "I'll even show you why." She handed her phone to Janey.

On the screen was a cat that had just one blue eye—the other side of his face was smooth fur, like Chester's. The cat in the photo looked happy, cuddled in the arms of a person who looked like a much younger Isabel.

"Is this Michou?" Janey asked. He was beautiful, and he also looked a little bit like someone had mixed Elsa and Chester together.

"That's him," Isabel confirmed. "Isn't he sublime?"

Janey's eyes lit up with happiness. They found a great home for Chester.

"Seeing these two felt a little bit like fate. Right, buddy?" Sam nuzzled the top of Chester's head, and Chester gave a very loud, very happy purr-ROW, which Elsa echoed, kneading Isabel's arm.

She nudged Kitty, giving her an enthusiastic nod. Kitty nodded back, and turned to the couple.

"You guys seem like you'll give them a

great home," she said, seeming to agree with Janey. "But I have to say, there's a problem here."

Janey's heart sank and she looked at Kitty, surprised. Sam and Isabel looked worried, too.

"You gave us too much money." Kitty laughed. "You only need to give us the adoption fee for one cat."

"Oh!" Sam grinned with relief. "That's intentional. We were always planning to pay both fees, and we have everything we need for Chester and Elsa at home already."

"We wanted to come to the shelter for Purr-fect Pairs so we could get a pair of cats who already knew and liked each other," Isabel explained. "Just like these two.

Consider the extra a donation."

"So wait," Janey said slowly, "does that mean . . . ?"

"Yes, Janey," Kitty said gently. "Chester is officially adopted, and so is Elsa. Congratulations on your new family members," she added to Sam and Isabel. "Just one thing left to do." It was her turn to nudge Janey.

"Oh!" Janey picked up her tablet, holding it up. "I want to get a picture for my blog!"

"Of course," Sam said, putting his arm around Isabel happily. "A family portrait!"

"Let's take one with the Pet Rescue Club, too," said Isabel, with a wink at Janey. "After all, without their help, we never would have known about Chester and Elsa at all."

A moment later, the members of the Pet Rescue Club were together, posing for a photo next to Elsa and Chester and their new family. "Say cheese!" said Kitty as she took the photo. She looked at the screen, then turned it around for the Rescue Club to see. "What do you think, guys?"

Janey looked happily at the photo, then up at Chester and Elsa with Sam and Isabel. "It's purr-fect," she said.

Food for Thought

We share a lot with our pets: our lives, our homes, our love, our deepest secrets. But is it a good idea to share our food?

Not always. Several common foods that are perfectly safe for people can be dangerous or even deadly for our cats, dogs, and other pets. Also, there are some household items and houseplants that pets should never be allowed to chew on or eat. Here are a few examples, but for a more complete list from the experts at the ASPCA, visit **aspca.org**.

- Onions and garlic

- Chocolate

- Coffee

- Avocado (especially dangerous to birds and rodents)

- Grapes and raisins

- Many human medications

- Antifreeze

- Fabric softener sheets

- Amaryllis

- Pothos (a popular houseplant)

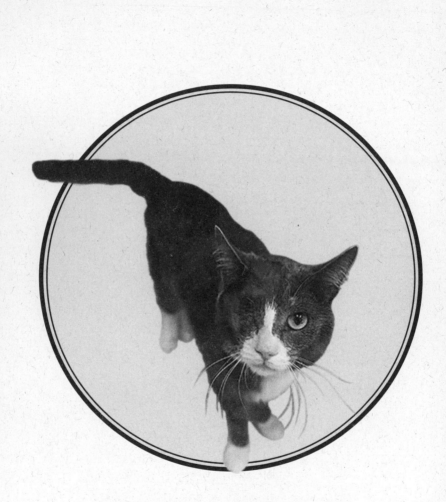

Meet the Real Chester

Chester from *A Purr-fect Pair* was inspired by an animal rescue story in New York! The real-life Chester had sustained a trauma before being rescued by the ASPCA and needed to have his right eye removed, but he was still gentle and quiet and playful.

When Christina and Jim came into the Adoption Center, they were looking for a perfect pair. First they spotted Elsa, a striking and sweet cat who wanted love immediately. Soon after, Chester, with his one-eyed stare, meowed and caught their attention, too. The two cats quickly became the best of friends just like the Elsa and Chester in our story.

Look for the books in the
PET RESCUE CLUB
series!

1 A New Home for Truman 2 No Time for Hallie

3 The Lonely Pony 4 Too Big to Run 5 A Puppy Called Disaster

6 Champion's New Shoes 7 A PURR-fect Pair 8 Bailey, the Wonder Dog